For Finn

BEACH LANE BOOKS · An imprint of Simon & Schuster Children's Publishing Division · 1230 Avenue of the Americas, New York, New York 10020 · Copyright © 2018 by Kimberly Gee · All rights reserved, including the right of reproduction in whole or in part in any form. · BEACH LANE BOOKS is a trademark of Simon & Schuster, Inc. · For information about special discounts for bulk purchases, please contact Simon & Schuster Special Sales at 1-866-506-1949 or business@simonandschuster.com. · The Simon & Schuster Speakers Bureau can bring authors to your live event. For more information or to book an event, contact the Simon & Schuster Speakers Bureau at 1-866-248-3049 or visit our website at www.simonspeakers.com. · Book design by Lauren Rille · The text for this book was set in Supernett. · The illustrations for this book were rendered in black Prismacolor and colored digitally. · Manufactured in China · 0818 SCP · First Edition · 10 9 8 7 6 5 4 3 2 1 · CIP data for this book is available from the Library of Congress. · ISBN 978-1-4814-4971-7 (hardcover) · ISBN 978-1-4814-4972-4 (eBook)

Mad, Mad Bear!

KIMBERLY GEE

Beach Lane Books
New York   London   Toronto   Sydney   New Delhi

Bear is mad.

He was the first one to have
to leave the park for a nap.

He got an owie
on the way home.

And then he had to take off his boots
and leave his favorite stick outside.

Bear thinks it is all no fair.

And that makes him very . . .

very . . .

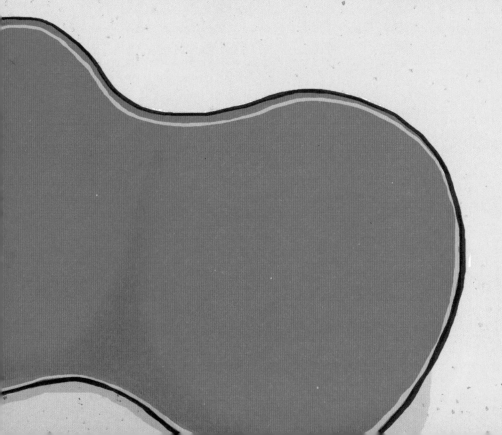

GRAAAAA

But then . . .

Bear takes a breath.

And another breath.

And another breath.

And then,
Bear lets it all go.

Now Bear feels quiet.

And a little hungry.

And a little sleepy.

When Bear wakes up, he feels all better!

He puts on his boots
and picks up his stick.

And goes back outside to play.